Ricardo and the Fisherman

Written and Illustrated by Joan Eiseman

MARBLE HOUSE EDITIONS

Published by Marble House Editions
96-09 66th Avenue (Suite 1D)
Rego Park, NY 11374

Library of Congress Cataloguing-in-Publication Data
Eiseman, Joan
Ricardo and the Fisherman/by Joan Eiseman

Summary: A folktale about a wealthy landowner in 17th century Spain who holds a contest to find the best chef in the world, one who can get his son to eat.

ISBN 0-9786745-4-5
Library of Congress Catalog Card Number 2007925489

Printed in China

For Eddie

Don Pedro Alvarado de Catalán was the richest man in all of Spain. He lived in a magnificent palace in the hills of Cádiz with his beautiful wife, Caterina di Napoli, and his handsome young son, Ricardo.

Don Pedro's lands spread as far as the eye could see. He had farmlands and vineyards, herds of cattle and sheep. He had a house near the seashore and several more all over Spain. Hundreds of Don Pedro's ships sailed the seas, making Don Pedro fabulously wealthy. From the Old World to the New and back, they carried spices and chocolate, gold and diamonds, livestock, grain, exotic fruits and flowers. Because Don Pedro's fleet of ships opened trade to the newly discovered Americas, the King of Spain owed much to him and considered him a good friend.

Every night, Don Pedro and Doña Caterina would host lavish banquets for the many important people who visited the palace. Diplomats, sea captains, kings and queens — all of them came to the shimmering palace of the famous Don Pedro. And oh, what evenings they had! They enjoyed the very best food and drink, storytelling, music and dancing.

Young Ricardo loved these feasts. He would stay up late into the night to hear all kinds of tales about the lost lands of Atlantis, the riddles of the sphinx and the pyramids of Egypt. He would drink in stories about the native peoples of the New World, with its treasures of gold, colorful birds, and strange ceremonies of hidden civilizations. He loved to hear about the vast continent of Africa, its tall Watusi tribesmen and tiny pygmy warriors. One day he would go to the jungles and savannahs of Africa to see those lions, tigers, and leopards, lively little monkeys and towering great apes.

When travelers would tell Ricardo their stories, he would always forget about eating his food. His mother would remind him to eat, but he was really more interested in hearing about magic carpets and genies in a bottle. Little Ricardo's head was so full of stories, and he had so many questions! How could his mother expect him to finish his food?

The family had an excellent chef who prepared the meals, but Doña Caterina was always complaining that her son would not eat. "He's too skinny!" she would say. But what could she do?

One day, Chef Pancho threw down his apron and told Doña Caterina that *she* could cook for Ricardo because *he* was going back home to Valencia. *Well*, Doña Caterina thought, *maybe that's the problem. My son needs his mother's cooking.* So she picked up the apron, put it on and started ordering all the kitchen helpers to clear the counter. They were going to make food that her own mother had made for her when she was growing up in Italy.

With much hustle and bustle, Doña Caterina turned flour and eggs into thin strands of spaghetti. She made tasty tomato and cheese sauce that she remembered from her childhood. She even invented a new dish, flattening out dough and topping it with tomato sauce and extra cheese. *Ricardo is going to love this*, she thought, happily. *I know why he never eats. He needs my special attention.*

At the next dinner party, the guests arrived, not knowing what the menu would be that night. Ricardo was excited as he watched his mother serve the spaghetti she had prepared herself, and he hoped he would be able to finish his food. He didn't feel all that hungry but he promised himself that he'd try.

Don Pedro was so proud of his wife! As he ate the spaghetti, he remembered how in love with her he was. The guests, too, twirled the long strands into their mouths and told Doña Caterina how delicious everything tasted.

What a success! All the serving platters were empty and all the food was gone! All, that is, except the food on Ricardo's plate, which had barely been touched.

"*Mi corazón*, you must eat," Doña Caterina said to her son. "You're just as skinny as a stick!"

"I did eat, and it was really good," Ricardo pleaded, before running off to play with his new kitten.

"Come back and finish the food your mother made!" Don Pedro shouted. But Ricardo was already gone.

Later that night, Doña Caterina cried and told her husband, "I failed, and our son will starve."

"No, Querida," he consoled her. "You are the best cook and Ricardo will be fine." But his words only made her cry more.

Don Pedro knew that if his wife wasn't happy, no one was going to be happy. So he made a plan. He would hold a contest to find the best chef in the whole world, one who could get Ricardo to eat. As a prize, the winner would receive his weight in gold and would become the family's personal chef.

The next morning Don Pedro told his wife his idea. She loved it. Ricardo did too. And so, messengers were sent out by land and sea with news about Don Pedro de Alvarado de Catalán's contest to find the world's greatest chef.

The news got out quickly, and soon the very popular Chef Rolando from nearby San Fernando came to the palace to enter the contest. He cooked a most delicious dish called *paella*, in which succulent pieces of chicken, sausage, and shrimp sat atop a bed of golden saffron rice. Heavenly! Next he prepared a coconut flan decorated with spun sugar and chocolate.

Chef Rolando was a true artist. Everyone praised his cooking and begged for more. Everyone except for Ricardo, who seemed busier feeding shrimp to his cat than eating his meal.

Don Pedro thanked Chef Rolando for his fine work but did not name him the winner because Ricardo had not eaten.

The next week, the fabulous Chef Marcel Gastrom, the number one genius of all French cooking, came to the palace. Don Pedro was honored. The ingredients on Gastrom's list were expensive, but Don Pedro did not mind. After all, it was for Ricardo.

In a whirlwind of activity, the Frenchman and his kitchen helpers set about to cut, cube, chop, slice and dice. Then they baked, basted, blended, boiled, sautéed and fried.

That evening, twenty hungry guests arrived. They feasted on fresh salads, creamy soup, a crispy fish dish, duck with cherries, and roasted meats, all followed by imported cheeses and ripe fruits. When everyone said they couldn't eat another bite, out came tiny cups of coffee and chocolate-filled pastries.

Not a crumb was left! Not a crumb, except on Ricardo's plate, which had barely been touched. Somehow by the end of the meal, he had disappeared. And so sadly, Chef Gastrom did not win the contest.

Many more fine chefs competed in the contest. There was Chef Alfonso de Goya, who prepared a mystery dish. It would be hot and cold and black and white, all at the same time. He told Don Pedro that no one who breathed air could resist this dish. The ingredients were even more expensive than Gastrom's but Don Pedro didn't mind. He thought to himself, *I can afford it. My son has to eat!*

After a whole day of working in the kitchen with mountains of ice, gallons of fresh milk, cream, sugar, and roasted cocoa beans, Alfonso presented that night's guests with his surprise. Out came the beautiful trays of frozen white sweet cream flavored with vanilla beans and hot, dark chocolate sauce. The whole confection with decorated with cherries, nuts and puffs of whipped cream. "Let's eat," announced Don Pedro.

Everyone dug in, and soon the room was filled with sounds like "Oooh," and "Ahhh," and comments like, "I must be dreaming," as the frozen cream melted into the chocolate sauce, creating a heavenly sensation.

Ricardo was very interested in knowing how the cocoa beans had been roasted but he barely touched his dish. And so once again, there was no winner.

By this time, the contest had become known worldwide. One chef came from India, bringing bags of rare spices: nutmeg, cinnamon and cardamom. His food was tasty, but too spicy. Another chef, traveling in a caravan along the Silk Road, decided to come all the way to Spain to try his luck.

Chef Ali would win the contest with his famous "March of the Flaming Shish-Kebabs." He sent waiters in turbans out of the kitchen with flaming swords of skewered meats. They danced around to belly dancing music, and when the flames died down, the waiters served the meat over beds of fluffy white rice. It was quite a show, but Ricardo hardly ate any of it.

Chefs came from Greece, Italy, Austria, and Morocco. It was all a lot of fun, but not one of them could get Ricardo to eat.

18

Finally, the famed chef Win Sing arrived in Cádiz at the port of Santa Maria with several chefs, 20 Chinese handmaidens, geese, ducks, turtles, and pigs. He announced that they would create for little Ricardo the grand Chinese New Year buffet that had been served to the Emperor of China.

Win Sing had brought all the ingredients with him on the clipper ship from China. There were special Chinese vegetables, soy sauces and spices. He didn't forget jasmine rice and cellophane noodles. He was prepared to win!

Each chef and the 20 beautiful Chinese handmaidens got right to work. There were going to be more than 30 different dishes with names like *Bird's Nest Soup, Thousand-Year-Old Eggs,* and *Seven-Jewel Rice.*

Everyone begged Don Pedro for an invitation to taste these wonders and Ricardo promised that he was going to eat everything. Guests started arriving at the palace, which had been decorated with Chinese lanterns and paper dragons. Elegantly dressed ladies, wealthy merchants, royalty, and other important people had come. Excitement was in the air as they smelled the rich and exotic food that had been prepared.

The beautiful handmaidens started bringing out fragrant bowls of jasmine rice, followed by platter after platter of fabulous surprises. Nobody knew the names of the food, but they ate and ate: lobster dishes, chicken dishes, beef dishes, pork and noodles, and shark fin soup. There were turtle egg pancakes with ginger and garlic, and fish glazed with bright red sauce. There were baby clams with black bean sauce and crab with vegetables.

Very soon, all the beef with orange and Peking duck disappeared. Fine ladies fought over the last of the shrimp, and elegant gentlemen grabbed the lobster tails.

Ricardo loved the Chinese banquet. He wanted to know the names of all the different foods. He wanted to hear about China. He was interested in everything that was going on except the eating part. He had barely tasted a thing! Again, there was no contest winner.

After the Chinese banquet, not one chef even tried to enter the competition. Then one day a handsome young man arrived at the palace door in hopes of entering the contest. It was Miguel, and Don Pedro recognized him at once as a fisherman from the village.

"Listen," Don Pedro said, "I am a very busy man and you are a fisherman, not a chef! So please don't waste my time."

Miguel was young but he was also not a fool, and he had a quick answer. "My Lord," he said humbly, "I will bet my fishing boat that I can win your contest."

"Will you?" replied Don Pedro with half a smile. "Well, I am a businessman, and if you lose the contest, I will surely take your boat! Tell me, do you still want to try?"

"Of course," said Miguel, with confidence. "I plan to take your son fishing with me. I will find out what he likes and I will make it for him."

By this time, Ricardo had become rather interested in this conversation. Miguel's idea sounded like fun!

"Yes!" he shouted. "That sounds great. Let's go!"

"Absolutely not!" Don Pedro said.

"Absolutely not!" said Doña Caterina.

Ricardo, who was used to getting his way, said, "Then I am never eating again!" Ricardo's parents didn't really believe him, but they also didn't want to take a chance.

"All right, " Doña Caterina agreed, "But please promise us that you will have our boy back here by sunset." The young fisherman promised that he would.

"And I also promise," he said, "that I will prepare a meal and Ricardo will eat everything."

"We'll see," said Don Pedro, happy that he was going to get Miguel's boat.

Miguel and Ricardo headed toward the sea with fishing poles and nets. At the shore, they spread out the nets and caught little sardines to use for bait.

When they had collected enough of the tiny fish, they climbed in Miguel's boat and rowed out to sea. Out in the deeper waters, Miguel showed the boy how to put the bait on the fishing pole and drop the line into the sea. Then they waited and waited, hoping to feel a tug on one of the lines. While they were waiting, they talked and laughed. Slowly, the fish started to bite. How exciting this was for Ricardo! He loved fishing.

Miguel and his little friend spent several hours out in the hot sun. Ricardo learned quickly that fishing took patience and hard work, but he was enjoying the thrill of seeing the fish get pulled in. He wanted to keep on fishing, but Miguel reminded him that he had promised Doña Caterina they'd be home before sunset. So before the sun started to go down, the two fishermen rowed back to shore.

Carrying their catch to Miguel's cottage, they chatted about what that night's dinner would be. "You can help me make the meal," Miguel told his young friend.

Ricardo helped Miguel carry buckets of water back and forth from the well. He collected firewood and then went into town to buy bread. After he came back, he went into the garden to look for wild strawberries. Meanwhile, in his kitchen, Miguel was frying up the fish and making a salad. When everything was ready, they loaded all the food onto Miguel's donkey and started the long walk to the palace.

About an hour later, they were approaching the palace door. In the doorway stood Don Pedro and Doña Caterina, who looked relieved to see their son again.

Miguel and Ricardo unloaded the food and brought it into the dining room, where the table was all ready. Together, they set out all the dishes of prepared food.

How lovely and tempting everything looked! Doña Caterina started nibbling on the freshly fried fish. "Very good," she said, approvingly.

Don Pedro munched on a crispy sardine. "Not bad," he admitted, thinking about his new boat.

Much to the amazement of his parents, Ricardo seemed very hungry and was excited to taste what he and Miguel had made. He filled up his plate and very quickly, the food was gone! Then he took a *second* helping!

Doña Caterina was happy to see her son eating with such gusto, but Don Pedro started thinking that maybe he would not get his boat....

When Ricardo finished the strawberry pie that Miguel had made, he said that he had never had such a good dinner. Don Pedro couldn't deny it – Miguel had won the contest.

He stood up, went over to him and shook his hand. "Young man," he said, "I congratulate you. You are the winner!"

"Thank you, my Lord," Miguel replied. "I am most honored."

"But how did you do it?" asked Don Pedro, bewildered.

"Sir," Miguel said, smiling, "it is not the food that has given your son an appetite. It is nothing more than a day's hard work. *That* is the secret."

From that day on, Ricardo spent his days learning from all the workers at the palace. He was a helper in the garden and in the kitchen, ran errands and best of all, fished with Miguel. And at the end of every day, he was delightfully tired and very, very hungry!

Miguel did get his weight in gold and became the palace chef. And together, the family of Don Pedro Alvarado de Catalán lived happily ever after, and ate very well, too!